For Layla Evie — G.M.

For Simone — S.M.K.

I am the lullaby

you are the melody

sing me

AN OLD BARN BOOK
First published in the UK in 2017 by Old Barn Books Ltd
West Sussex, England, RH20 1JW
www.oldbarnbooks.com

Distributed in the UK by Bounce Sales & Marketing

First published in Australia in 2017 by Allen & Unwin

ISBN: 978-1-910646-34-2

The artwork was created using watercolour and ink.
Cover and text design by STINGart
Set in Gurnsey and Dannette by STINGart
Colour reproduction by Splitting Image, Australia
This book was printed in May 2017 by C&C Offset Printing Co. Ltd, China.
10 9 8 7 6 5 4 3 2 1

GLENDA MILLARD   STEPHEN MICHAEL KING

Pea Pod
Lullaby

Old Barn
Books

I am the small green pea

you are the tender pod

hold me

I am the diving kite

you are the bow-tied tail

steady me

I am the drifting boat

you are the quiet deep

buoy me

I am the fleeting breath

shelter me

I am the falling star

you are the wishful hands

catch me

I am the windblown husk

you are the jewelled rain

quench me

I am the sapphire night

you are the lantern moon

light me

I am the looking-glass

you are the image there

see me

I am the tumbling leaf

you are the whispered breeze

dance me

I am the castaway

you are the journey's end

welcome me

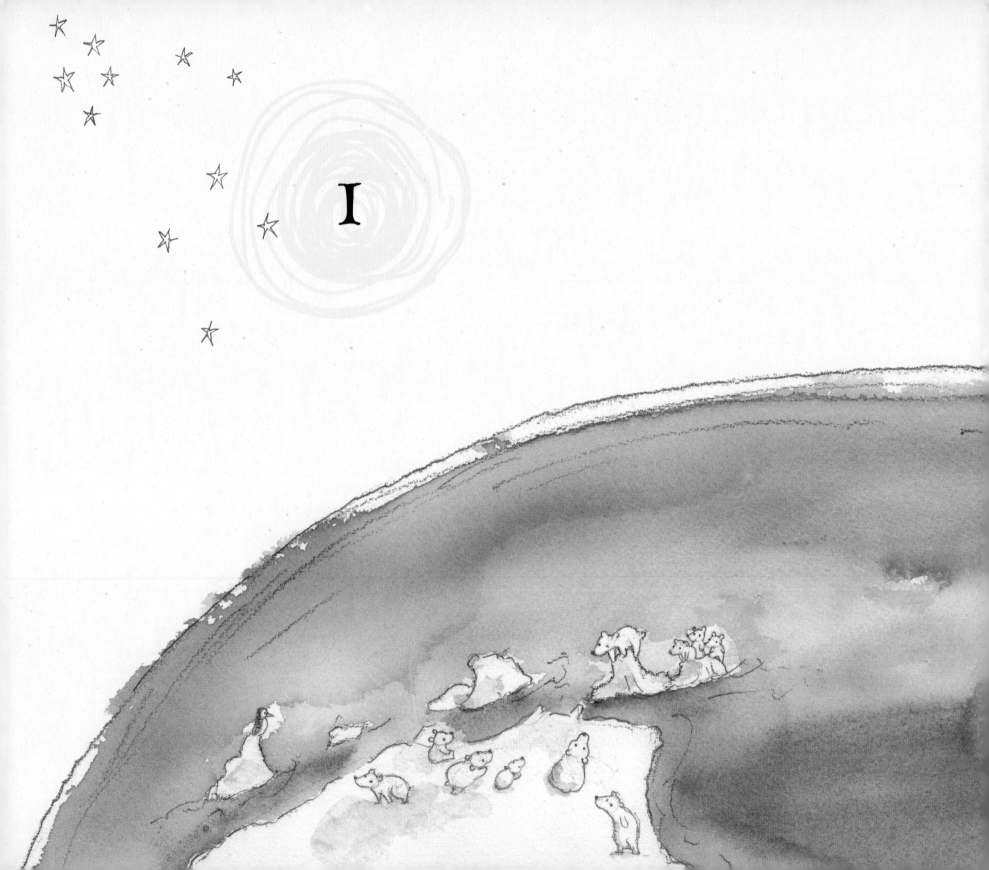

You

We

For Glenda Millard and Stephen Michael King the making of *Pea Pod Lullaby* was a particularly special experience. Glenda joined Stephen at the Manning Regional Art Gallery where Stephen was creating the initial illustrations for the book as part of the gallery's wall project. As Stephen drew the scenes, Glenda placed the verses, revising the words as the storyboard emerged. They made the book together, trusting each other with their newly formed ideas, and welcoming the comments of the people in the gallery who watched author and illustrator at work.

Glenda Millard is the author of many acclaimed novels and picture books, and Stephen Michael King has illustrated, written and designed many wonderful books for children. Their books include *The Duck and the Darklings* (Winner 2016 WA Premier's Book Awards, Children's Books, Shortlisted 2015 CBCA Picture Book of the Year, Shortlisted 2015 NSW Premier's Literary Awards, and a 2015 White Raven book), *Applesauce and the Christmas Miracle*, and *The Tender Moments of Saffron Silk* and other books in the Kingdom of Silk series.